T5-CVF-739

DOUBLE DOG DARE

Ray Prather

Double Dog Dare

MACMILLAN PUBLISHING CO., INC.
New York
COLLIER MACMILLAN PUBLISHERS
London

Copyright © 1975 Ray Prather
All rights reserved. No part of this book may be reproduced or transmitted in any form or by any means, electronic or mechanical, including photocopying, recording or by any information storage and retrieval system, without permission in writing from the Publisher.
Macmillan Publishing Co., Inc.
866 Third Avenue, New York, N.Y. 10022
Collier-Macmillan Canada Ltd.
Printed in the United States of America

1 2 3 4 5 6 7 8 9 10

Library of Congress Cataloging in Publication Data
Prather, Ray. Double dog dare.
(A Ready-to-read book) I. Title.
PZ7.P887Do [E] 74-13316 ISBN 0-02-775040-X

The three-color illustrations were prepared as black wash drawings, with overlays for brown and green. The typeface is Alphatype Century X, with the display set in Clarendon Regular.

For Susan and Ada

"Look what I found, Rudy.
A quarter."

"Halfers, halfers."

"Nope, finders keepers."

"What're you going to buy, Eddie?"

"Ice cream."

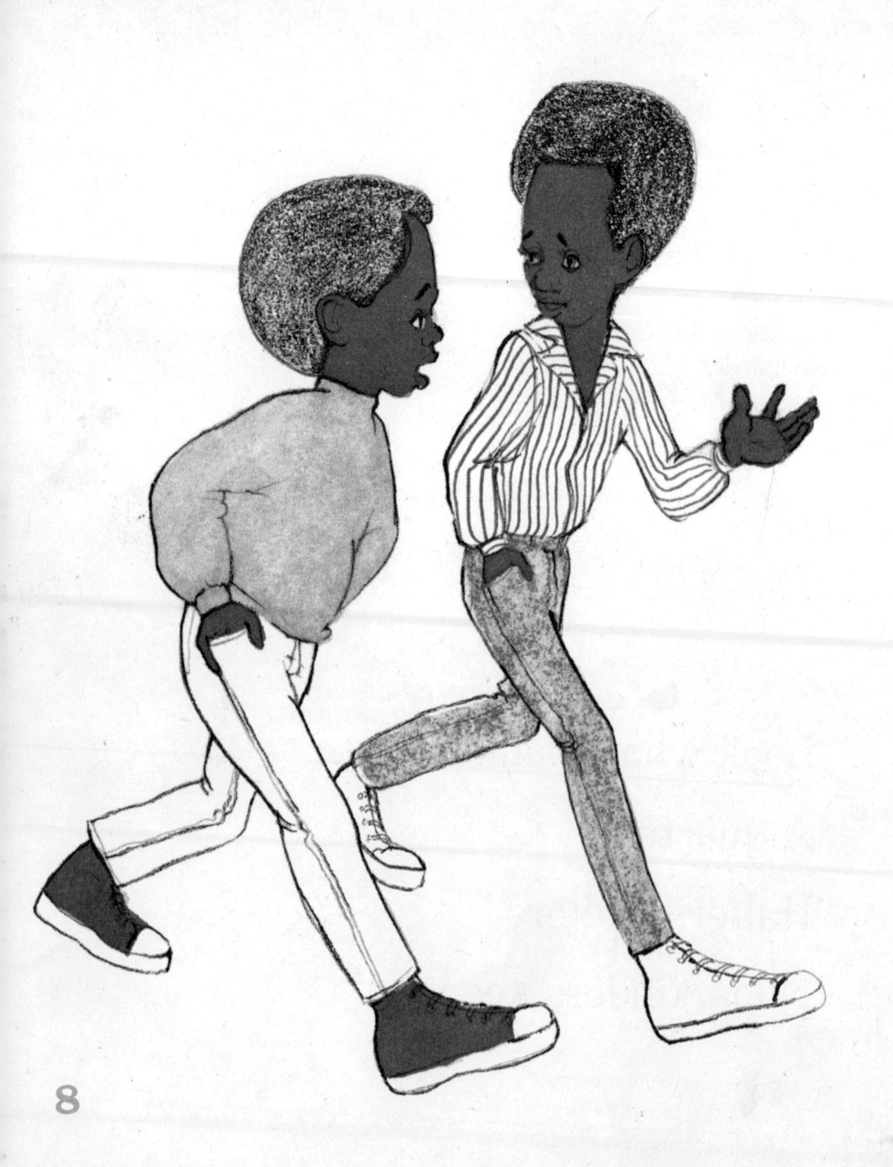

“Get strawberry.”

“Nope, I like chocolate.

And it’s my quarter.”

"Come on, give me a lick."

"You just wait, Rudy."

“Hurry up.

You’ve had six licks already.”

“Okay, here.

“Hey, that’s enough. Watch it, Rudy.

Lick over here some. Now…now…now.

That was six already."

"I know. I can count."

CRUNCH!

"Look what you've done, Rudy."

"You should have let me hold it, Eddie.
You held it too hard."

"No, I didn't. You licked it too hard."

"No, I didn't."

"Yes, you did.
You'd better get me an ice cream.
OR ELSE!!"

"Eddie, don't. It was an accident.

I'm getting tired, Eddie.

Quit! I said it was an accident.

Now quit!!"

"Let's go find another quarter, Eddie."

"That's silly, Rudy.

It'll never happen again.

And you know it."

"Come on. Race you up that tree."

"I dare you to do this, Eddie."

"Shucks, that's easy, man."

"Look! There's Miss Riley's house.
Mine's right over there. See?"

"Hee, hee. It's upside down.
Keep climbing.
That's not the top.
Wheeeeeeeeee...."

"See, that was nothing, Rudy.
Watch out! That limb is too skinny.
Hey, there's some mistletoe.
Do you know
what that's used for?"
"Sure, Eddie."
"What?"
"Kissing—ughh!
Let's climb down
and do something else."

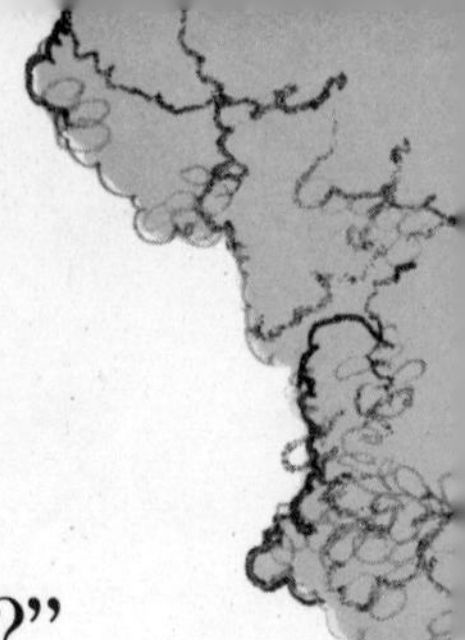

"Hey, whose dog is that, Rudy?"

"I don't know.

Go away, dog. Get!"

"He's not getting."

"Yeah, he looks kind of mean, too.

What're we going to do, Eddie?"

"Stay up in this tree, that's what.

Anything in your pockets, Rudy?"

"Nope. Why?"

"If I throw something,

maybe he'll run after it."

"Break off a stick.

“He still didn’t move, Eddie.
And he didn’t pay any attention
to that stick, either.

Let’s growl at him.

He might scare.

"Grrrrrrrrrrr...Grrrrrrrrr...."

"He's not afraid of that, Rudy.

You sound like a puppy, anyway."

"You think we'll have to stay
up here all night, Eddie?"

"Nope. I've got to get home
for supper."

"Well, we aren't going anywhere
until he leaves.
And he's not moving."

"I'm hungry."

"Me too. I double-dog-dare you to go first."

"Nope...uh...ughhh.... Darers go first."

"I sure am tired of this old tree."

"Yeah, me too.
 Why doesn't he go?
 What does he want with us?"

"Here, Queenie, here, Queenie!!
Come here, Queenie!"

“Is that your dog?”

“Yes, she is.”

“You shouldn’t let her go
around biting people.”

“She didn’t bite you.”

“Well, she could have.”

“But she didn’t. She’s a nice dog.

She doesn't bite."

"She tried to. She was growling
mean at us."

"No, she wasn't. She only wanted
to play with you."

"You call that playing?
Come on, Rudy."

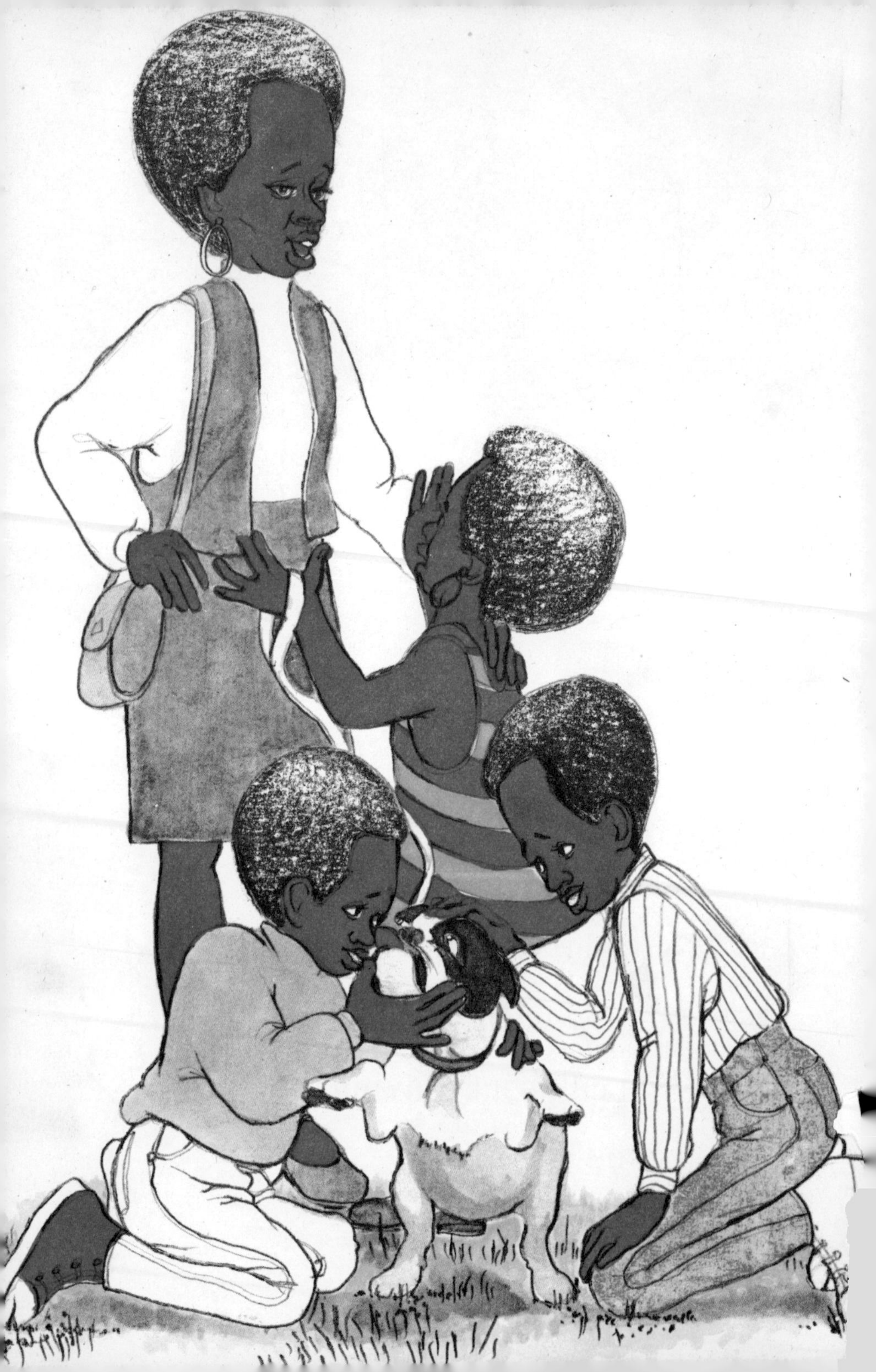

“Oh, Susan, your two friends
have found Queenie.”

“But, Ma....”

“Why don’t you thank them?”

“But, Ma....”

“I think they deserve some
ice cream.”

“Yes, ma’am. We do.”

“I deserve some strawberry.”

“And I deserve some chocolate.
Queenie sure is a nice dog.”

"See, Eddie?

You've got your ice cream."

"Hee, hee, yeah. Want a lick?"

"Nope, I've got my own.

STRAWBERRY!!!"

c, 2

GM

FAIRFAX COUNTY PUBLIC LIBRARY
FAIRFAX, VIRGINIA 22030

GM

E
c.2

Prather, Ray
Double dog dare. Macmillan, 1975.
(Ready-to-read)
533

I. Title.